STEP 2:
Run a piece of string through the holes, and tie the string in the back. Now you have your very own Agent P mask!

D0517524

THE MISSING PLATYPUS

Adapted by Ellie O'Ryan
Based on the series created by Dan Povenmire & Jeff "Swampy" Marsh

Printed in the United States of America   First Edition   1 3 5 7 9 10 8 6 4 2

ISBN 978-1-4231-6821-8

J689-1817-1-12122

For more Disney Press fun, visit www.disneybooks.com

Disney Press
New York

PHINEAS AND FERB were about to set off on the family vacation of a lifetime—a trip to an animal research station in Africa! Their dad's friend Ignatius had invited the boys' friends along, too.

"I bet Perry's looking forward to meeting all of the wild animals . . . from a safe distance, of course," Phineas told Ferb.

Suddenly, Perry's watch started beeping. In addition to being Phineas and Ferb's pet platypus, he was a spy known as Agent P.

"I'm afraid you're going to have to miss your family vacation," Major Monogram said, appearing on the watch's screen. "You know we wouldn't do this if it weren't an emergency."

Agent P knew he had to act fast. He suddenly started to cough and sneeze.

"Oh no, I think he's sick," Phineas commented.

"He doesn't look well enough to travel," Phineas's mom said.

Phineas and Ferb hated to leave Perry behind. But they knew their mom was right.

As soon as he could slip away, Agent P dashed off to his lair for more information. But it turned out that the emergency wasn't so urgent after all.

"Why don't you check in on Dr. Doofenshmirtz anyway?" Major Monogram suggested.

Something wasn't right at Doofenshmirtz Evil, Incorporated. Even though the wicked doctor trapped Perry right away, Agent P broke free almost immediately.

Then, Dr. Doofenshmirtz purposely hit the self-destruct button on his latest -inator!

Since nothing *too* evil seemed to be taking place at Doofenshmirtz Evil, Inc., Agent P left. But that was all part of the doctor's plan.

"Ha! Perry the Platypus is out of the picture!" he shouted to his robot, Norm. "Behold! The Ultimate Evil-inator! With this, I'll blast Major Monogram, turning him . . . evil!"

Dr. Doofenshmirtz knew that at around this time every day, Major Monogram went up to his roof to sunbathe. At that moment, the doctor pushed a button on his -inator, zapping Major Monogram's headquarters with a beam of pure evil!

But the beam didn't hit Major Monogram. It hit Carl Karl the intern instead!

Meanwhile, Phineas and the gang had just arrived in Africa. Ignatius took everybody on a wild safari, where they saw herds of exotic animals.

"Awesome!" everyone exclaimed.

The last stop on the safari was a mysterious gorge.
"What's down there?" Phineas asked.
"Your guess is as good as mine," Ignatius replied. "In order to get down there, you would need a highly unconventional vehicle."
That gave Phineas an idea!

Back in Danville, Dr. Doofenshmirtz started moving his things into Major Monogram's agency headquarters.

"Feels good, doesn't it?" Dr. Doofenshmirtz commented. "Being evil!"

"What are you talking about?" Major Monogram asked.

"You've been zapped by my Ultimate Evil-inator!" the doctor shouted. "If you're not evil . . . then who is?"

Slam! Suddenly, a large trap fell over Major Monogram and Dr. Doofenshmirtz!

"Ha, ha!" Carl laughed. *"I'm going to take over the Tri-State Area. With my administrator's access to the supercomputer and intimate knowledge of proper photocopying techniques, I'm just the unpaid stooge to do it!"*

"Don't worry! I have more in the truck!" Dr. Doofenshmirtz cried. The intern ordered him to go outside and get them. With Carl distracted, no one noticed that Major Monogram was building a top secret communications device!

Moments later, Agent P received a transmission on his watch.
"Something terrible has happened," Major Monogram said in an urgent whisper. "Listen carefully—" Then the transmission went dead!
Agent P zoomed over to the spy agency headquarters. But before he could free Major Monogram, he was snagged in a trap!

Dr. Doofenshmirtz couldn't believe that his evil plan was ruined. At that moment, he leaned against the wall . . . and accidentally released Agent P!

   Finally, Phineas and Ferb's highly unconventional vehicle was ready to launch! With Phineas at the control panel and Ferb manning the wheel, the group headed toward the gorge.
   "First, we'll fly down like a graceful condor, landing on that rock outcropping," Phineas explained. "Then, we will jump over to those vines. Buford, Baljeet, you guys have the legs."

"Move over," Buford growled to Baljeet. "This is *obviously* a job for rash, unthinking muscle." He grabbed the lever with so much force that he ripped it right off the control panel!

The vehicle wobbled back and forth. Then it plunged off the ledge—right toward the gorge below!

At the spy agency headquarters, Agent P quickly disabled the supercomputer so that Carl would never be able to use its power for evil.

"Get him!" Carl shouted to Dr. Doofenshmirtz.

"I've got an idea!" Dr. Doofenshmirtz exclaimed. He raced from one -inator to the next, turning all of them on at once.

Carl ordered Dr. Doofenshmirtz to stop immediately. But it was too late.

Zzzzzzap! Suddenly, a blinding flash of light ripped through the room as all the -inators blasted Agent P!

"Where in the world is Perry?" Major Monogram cried. The platypus had vanished!

If someone could figure out which -inator had zapped Agent P first, maybe they could bring him back. But how in the world would they find him?

And what was going to happen to Phineas and the gang as they fell deeper into the gorge?